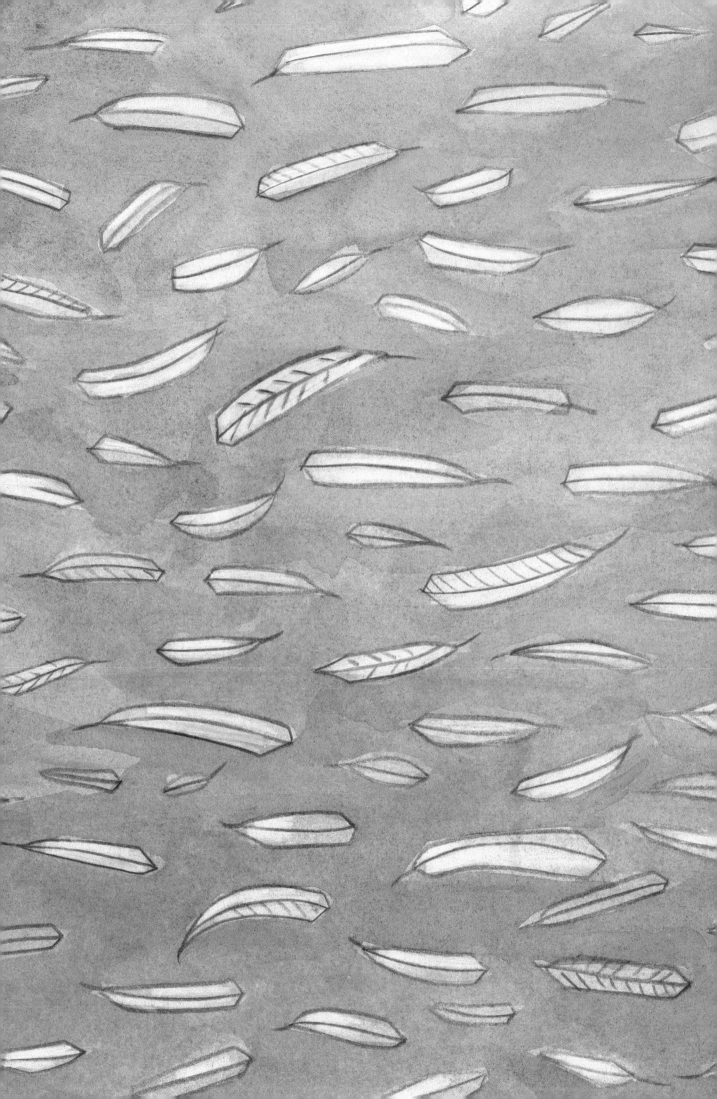

For Hamish.
Your light still burns bright,
little one. I carry it always.

—R.N.

E
467-0652

www.enchantedlion.com

First edition published in 2018 by Enchanted Lion Books,
67 West Street, 317A, Brooklyn, NY 11222
Text copyright © 2018 by Rachel Noble
Illustrations copyright © 2018 by Zoey Abbott
A CIP record is on file with the Library of Congress. ISBN 978-1-59270-239-8

Printed in China by RR Donnelley Asia Printing Solutions Ltd.

First Printing

Finn's
Feather

Rachel Noble   Zoey Abbott

ENCHANTED LION BOOKS
NEW YORK

On the first day of spring,

Finn opened the front door and discovered a feather on his doorstep.

It was white, it was amazing, it was perfect.

Finn ran to his mom, bubbling with excitement.

"Look what I found!"

"That's a lovely feather," said Mom.

"It's not just any feather, Mom. Hamish sent it."

Mom took a deep breath and gave him a great, big hug.

"Hamish is always with you. Feather or no feather," she said.

Finn thought his mom would be more excited about the feather.

It was definitely from Hamish.

Finn took the feather to school to show his teacher.

"Hamish left me a feather!"

Mrs. Gilbert took a deep breath and gave Finn a great, big smile.

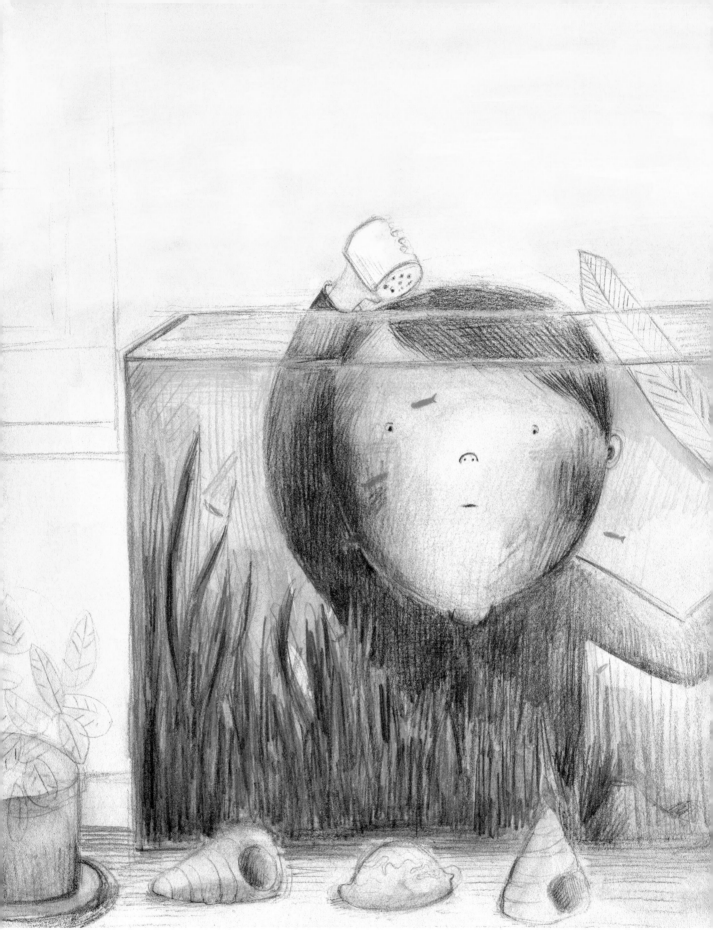

Finn was confused.

Why was he the only one excited about his feather?
Couldn't anyone else see how white, amazing, and perfect it was?

At lunchtime, Finn and his friend Lucas sat down together.

"What have you got?" Lucas asked.

"A feather. I think my brother Hamish sent it."

"Really? Angels can do that?" asked Lucas.

"I think they can," said Finn.

"It's a nice feather."

"It's amazing!"

They packed up their lunch, ready to play.
"What are you going to do with the feather?" asked Lucas.

Finn shrugged.

"I mean, why did Hamish give it to you?"

"Maybe he wanted to say hi," said Finn.

"Or maybe he wanted you to have fun with it?"
Lucas smiled, a sparkle in his eye.

"I know!" said Finn. "Let's make the biggest castle
in the whole world and stick the feather on top!"

Everyone gathered around and admired the friends' creation.
Finn's feather shimmered in the sunlight.

"What should we do next?" Finn was ready.

"I know!" cried Lucas, his eyes sparkling even brighter.

They chased each other around and around the playground.

The feather was better than fingers and made them laugh really hard.

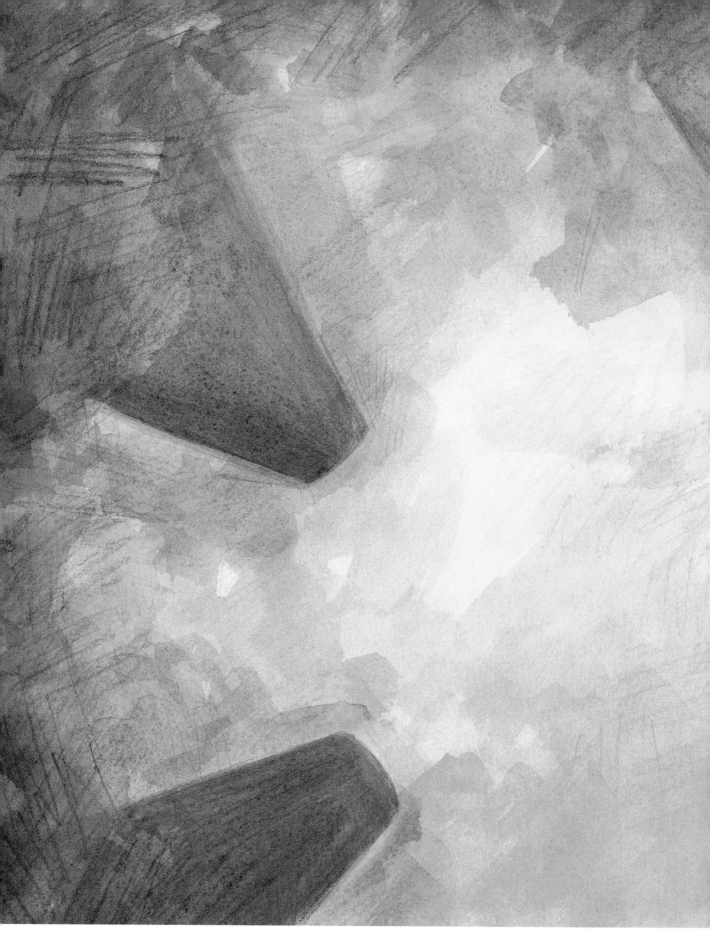

"This feather is the best!" said Lucas. "It's so great that Hamish left it for you. He's a really cool angel."

"He was a really cool brother. I miss him."
Finn ran his finger down the spine of the feather,
happy to have his friend at his side.

Moments later, a gust of wind whisked the feather
out of Finn's hands.

The feather soared over their castle and across the playground,
finally getting caught in the branches of a tree.
The boys looked at each other in despair.

"Come on everyone!" Lucas whistled across the playground,
calling their friends over to help.

1, 2, 3! The friends lifted Finn as high as they could,
  until the feather tickled the tips of his fingers.
"Almost there!" Lucas cheered.

"Woo Hoo!" they all shouted as Finn jumped down,
holding the feather like a trophy.

"What should we do with it now?" Lucas turned to his friend.

"Hold it tight," said Finn.

After school, Finn walked home with his mom,
his heart lighter, his smile wider.
"I had such a fun time with the feather!" Finn exclaimed.

"Thanks Hamish" he whispered.

Mom took a deep breath, smiled, and gave him a great, big hug.

The feather was no longer white. No longer perfect.

But it was still amazing.

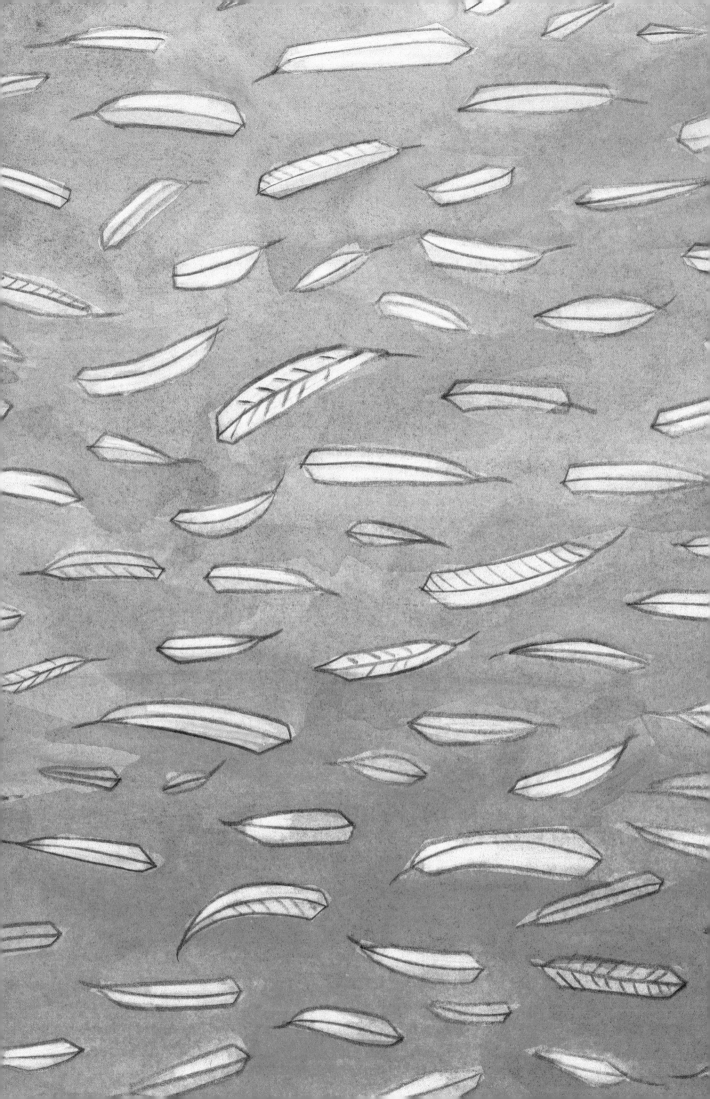